susannc n sage

teddybears and the cold cure

This edition first published in paperback in 1998
by A & C Black (Publishers) Ltd
35 Bedford Row
London WC1R 4JH
Reprinted 1998, 2000

ISBN 0-7136-5023-0

First published in 1984 by Ernest Benn Limited
Second impression published by
A & C Black (Publishers) Ltd
Reprinted 1993

A CIP catalogue record for this book is available from the British Library.

Printed in Singapore by Imago Publishing Ltd.

A & C BLACK • LONDON

"I feel ill," said William.
"You can't be ill," said Andrew;
"we're going to try out our new tools."

"But I *am* ill,"
said William,
"and I'm going to bed."

William's breakfast was still on the table.

"Perhaps he really is ill," said Robert.
"Don't you believe it," said Louise;
"he just wants breakfast in bed."
"Let's go and see," said Charles.

William sat up.
"You don't look so ill to me," said Louise.
"My throat hurts," William complained.

That afternoon, William was still in bed.
"Let's play *Pig in the Middle* to cheer you up," said Andrew.
"My head hurts," said William.

Next morning, Charles made a special breakfast.

"I'm not hungry," said William.

"But William is always hungry," said Louise.

"He *must* be ill."

Charles found a thermometer.
Louise took out her torch.
"You've got white spots on your throat,
William," she said.
"And he's got a temperature, too," said Charles.
"We'll have to look after him."

Louise and John made the bed.
Robert fetched a hot water bottle.
"I'll be in charge of the temperature chart," said Charles.
Andrew made a honey-and-lemon drink.
"Thank you," croaked William.

In the evening,
William felt worse.
One minute
he was boiling hot;
the next,
he was cold as ice.
His sheets were sticky
and talking gave him
a headache.
The other bears tiptoed
away, and at last
William fell asleep.

What was that?
Tap-tap. Tap-tap-tap.
William sat bolt upright.
“GO AWAY!” he shouted.

Suddenly, the light went on.
"I heard something tapping," said William.
"It must have been the wind," said Robert.
"And I *saw* things," said William.
"It's because you're ill," said Charles.

The next day,
there was a chocolate pig for William,
and Sara brought him some flowers.
"I hope you like tulips," she said.
Charles gave him a bell.
"Ring if you need anything,"
he said.
"Thank you," said William;
and for the next few days
he stayed in bed.

Then one morning, Sara made some porridge.
"Thank you," said William.
"But could you get me a banana milkshake?
For my throat."

Robert brought him
some apples.
"Thank you,"
said William;
"but will you
peel one for me?"

Andrew brought him some cards.
"Thank you," said William.
"But I'd rather have a new jigsaw puzzle . . .
and a bag of peanuts."
"Hmm," said Louise.

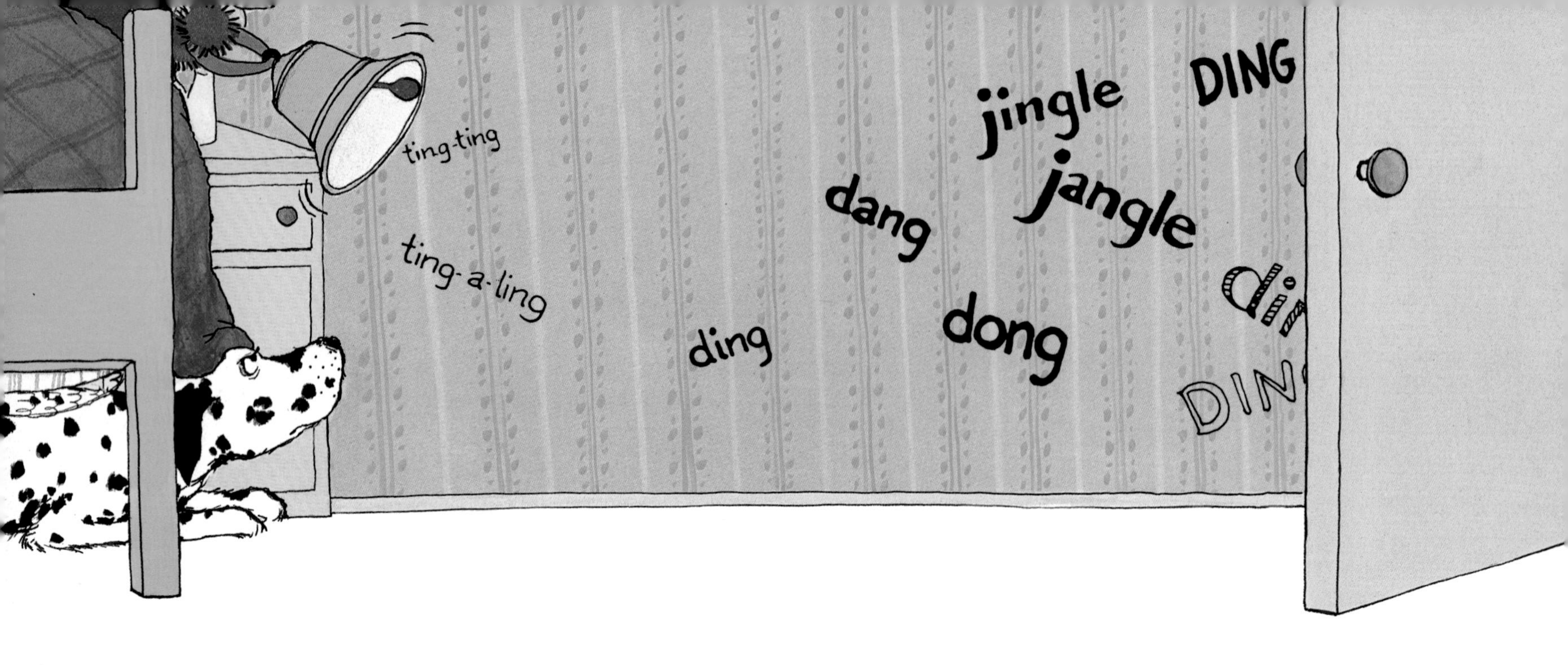

Before long, William remembered his bell.
"Sara," he called. "Could you bring me a blanket?"
He rang his bell again.
"Charles! Robert! Can you open the window? It's too hot now."
William's bell rang once more.
"John! Will you read me a story?"

William's bell was still ringing.
"What does he want *now*?"
said Andrew.
"He wants a bag of chips," said Louise.
"Who's going to get them?" said Sara;
"it's cold outside and –
look! It's snowing."

"They're very quiet downstairs," thought William. "Where's my lunch?" He looked out of the window.

There they were!
Out in the snow.

William waited and waited.
At last Louise came in with a tray.
“Where are my chips?” said William crossly.
“Sorry,” said Louise,
“but we made rice pudding instead.
It’ll be better for your throat.”

Andrew put his head round the door.
"Come on, Louise. We're ready now."
"Ready for *what*?" said William.
"We'll tell you later," said Louise,
"when we've finished."

JIGSAW
100 pieces
TISSUES
Wishing you a speedy recovery–
Good

William looked at the rice pudding.
Then he looked at his jigsaw;
but the bits would not stay together
and there were crumbs *everywhere*.
"Where *is* everyone?" he wondered.

CRASH! clatter clatter THUMP.

"What's that?" said William.
Then there was the sound of sawing.

screeeee-
scrawww
screeeee-
scrawww

"They're making something!"
said William.

Was it a shelf?
A letterbox? A birdhouse?
. . . a giant birdhouse?

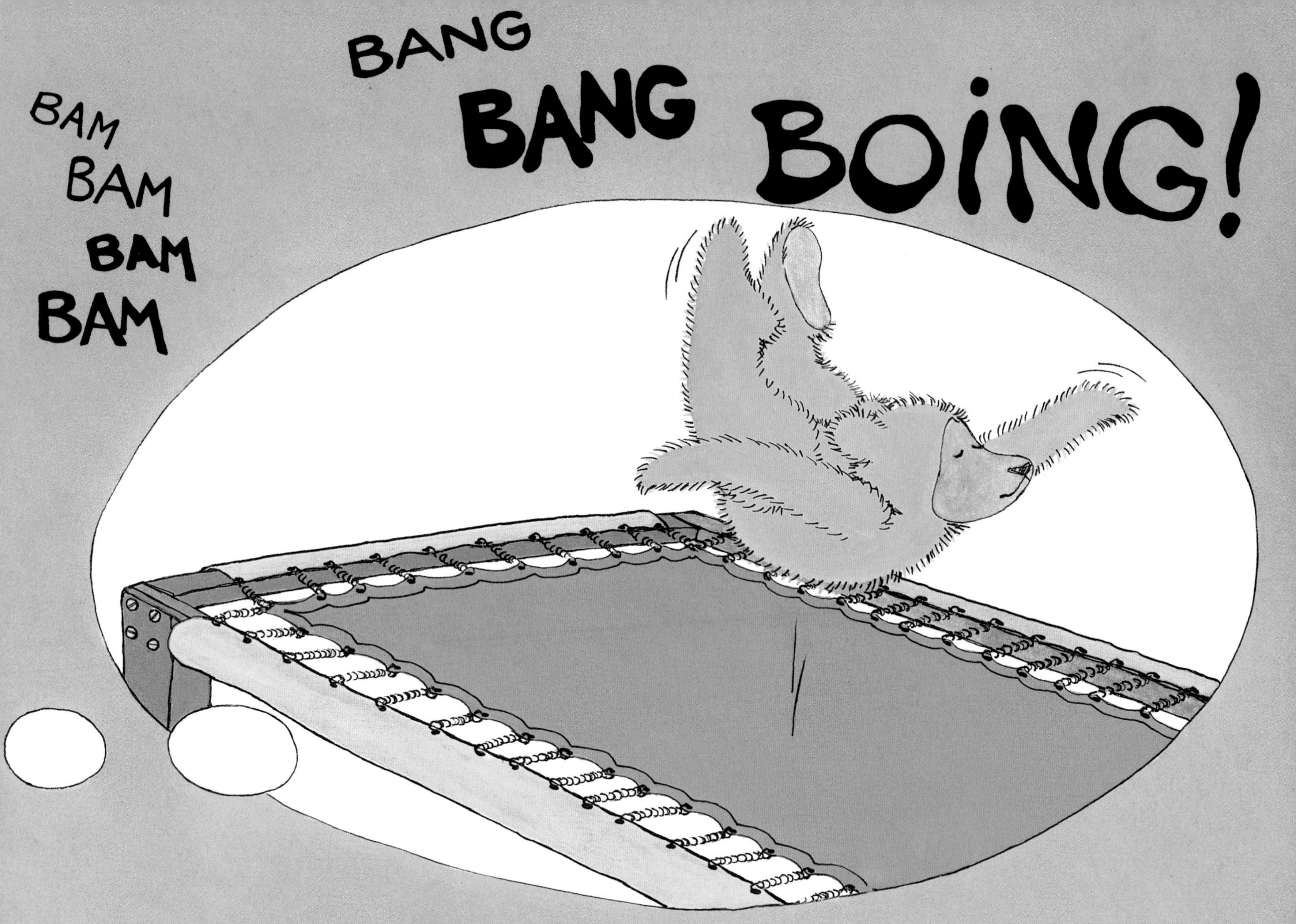

. . . a trampoline?
William could stand it no longer.
He jumped out of bed and ran downstairs.

"Nobody in the kitchen?" thought William.
"What are you doing out of bed?" said the others, appearing all at once.
"Have you seen what we've made?"
William's mouth was too full to answer.
"Come and see," said Sara.

It was a sledge!

“Who’s going to steer first?”
said Louise.
“I am,” said William.
“But you’re ill,” said Louise.
“I *was* ill,” corrected William.
“I’m feeling perfectly well now, thank you.”

All afternoon they went sledging
until it began to get dark.

"Tea time," said William. Everyone was hungry, except for Louise.
"But there's doughnuts and chocolate cake," said William.
"I don't want any tea and I'm going home to bed," said Louise.
"I think I'm ill."